"Save Mr. Lizard! Save Mr. Lizard!"

"We have something for Mr. Lizard," Karen Koombs said to the security guard at the TV station. She held out the envelope containing the petition.

"I'll take it," a woman said. "I'm Jane, the producer of the show."

"And I'm that other guy," a man with bright red hair said with a wink.

"It's him!" Bess squealed under her breath. "It's Mr. Lizard."

Nancy and her friends hurried out of the station and onto the sidewalk. Nancy felt very proud—until the doors swung open and Mr. Lizard marched out.

"Is this some kind of joke?" Mr. Lizard asked. He reached into the envelope and pulled out a sheet of notebook paper.

Everyone gasped. Written on it in big purple letters were the words "Get rid of Mr. Lizard!!"

The Nancy Drew Notebooks

Available from MINSTREL Books

THE
NANCY DREW
NOTEBOOKS®

#44

The Purple Fingerprint

CAROLYN KEENE
ILLUSTRATED BY JAN NAIMO JONES

A
MINSTREL®
BOOK

Published by POCKET BOOKS
New York London Toronto Sydney Singapore

A MINSTREL PAPERBACK *Original*

A Minstrel Book published by
POCKET BOOKS, a division of Simon & Schuster, Inc.
1230 Avenue of the Americas, New York, NY 10020

Copyright © 2001 by Simon & Schuster, Inc.

ISBN: 0-7434-0692-3

First Minstrel Books printing October 2001

10 9 8 7 6 5 4 3 2 1

NANCY DREW, THE NANCY DREW NOTEBOOKS, A MINSTREL BOOK and colophon are registered trademarks of Simon & Schuster, Inc.

For information regarding special discounts for bulk purchases, please contact Simon & Schuster Special Sales at 1-800-456-6798 or business@simonandschuster.com

Cover art by Joanie Schwarz

Printed in the U.S.A.

PHX/✠

1

Bad News Brenda

Macaroni and cheese, please!" eight-year-old Nancy Drew called out from the lunch line.

"For all of us!" Bess Marvin said.

George Fayne gave Bess a nudge.

"—Please!" Bess added quickly.

Bess and George were Nancy's two best friends. They were also cousins who looked very different. George—whose real name was Georgia—had brown eyes and dark curly hair. Bess had blue eyes and long blond hair.

But all three friends had a lot in common. They were in Mrs. Reynolds's third-grade class at Carl Sandburg Elementary School. And they couldn't wait for macaroni-and-cheese Monday.

Mrs. Enid Carmichael, the lunch lady, stood behind the counter. She wore her usual pink uniform and a hairnet.

"Sorry, girls," Mrs. Carmichael said. "No macaroni and cheese today."

Nancy couldn't believe her ears. "But it's Monday," she said, surprised.

"And I said 'please,'" Bess said.

Mrs. Carmichael smiled.

"Today we're having something from my brand-new cookbook," she said. "It's a French dish called quiche à la fromage."

"Keesh a la . . ." Nancy tried to say.

"I hope that's French for macaroni and cheese," George said.

Mrs. Carmichael pointed to a board hanging on the wall. It was where she wrote the lunch menu in bright purple marker.

"There'll be something new and yummy

each day this week," Mrs. Carmichael said.

Nancy brushed aside her reddish blond bangs. She read the lunch board.

"Stuffed hard-boiled eggs with mushrooms?" Nancy gasped.

"Zucchini pie?" Bess squeaked.

"Those sound like something Dalton Feivish would whip up for the science fair," George said.

Nancy nodded. Dalton Feivish was in Mrs. Apple's third-grade class. He was famous for his gross science projects.

"I heard that!" a voice snapped.

Nancy, Bess, and George turned around. Standing behind them was Dalton!

"Excuse me, Mrs. Carmichael," Dalton called over the girls' shoulders. "Do you have any *moldy* bread in your kitchen?"

"I should say not!" Mrs. Carmichael declared. "All my bread is fresh!"

"Too bad." Dalton sighed. "For my next experiment I was going to grow mold inside my gym socks."

"Eww!" Nancy and her friends cried at the same time.

The girls placed their plates on their trays and hurried to a table.

"Okay," George said, staring at her plate. "Who's going to try it first?"

"Nancy's a detective," Bess said quickly. "She can solve the mystery of the weird-looking lunch."

"Thanks a lot!" Nancy joked.

But Bess was right. Nancy loved solving mysteries. She even had a blue detective notebook where she wrote all of her clues.

Nancy took a deep breath. She tasted the lunch with the funny name and smiled.

"This is yummy!" she said. "Sort of like a cheesy-tasting pie."

Suddenly Bess began to laugh.

"I just remembered when Mr. Lizard pretended to cook on his show," Bess said.

Nancy grinned. *Mr. Lizard's Funhouse* was their favorite TV show after school. Mr. Lizard had bright red hair and did the funniest things. He had even made up his own lizard dance.

"I remember, too!" Nancy exclaimed. "Mr. Lizard was trying to cook fudge."

"Except it looked more like *sludge!*" George giggled.

The friends began to laugh—until Brenda Carlton sat down next to them.

"I know something you don't know," she began to sing softly.

Nancy rolled her eyes. Brenda Carlton thought she knew everything. Her father owned a newspaper, and she even wrote her own, called the *Carlton News,* on her computer every week.

"*Mr. Lizard's Funhouse* will *not* be on TV anymore," Brenda announced.

Nancy almost dropped her fork. "How do you know?" she asked.

"My father told me so," Brenda said. "The TV station is putting a cooking show on instead. Something called *The Clever Cook.*"

"A cooking show?" George complained.

"That's for grown-ups!" Bess cried.

Nancy wondered if Brenda was telling the truth. She had made up stories before.

"Maybe it's not true," Nancy said.

"Are you calling me a liar?" Brenda demanded.

"Nope," George joked. "We already call you Miss Snooty Pants."

"Very funny," Brenda muttered.

Nancy turned to Bess and George.

"Let's ask someone who will know for sure," she said. "Like Karen Koombs. She's the president of the Mr. Lizard Fan Club."

"Good idea," George said. "We can go to Karen's house after school. That's where she has the fan club meetings."

Brenda rolled her eyes.

"Good luck," she said. "The Mr. Lizard Fan Club doesn't want third graders. They wouldn't let me join."

Brenda flipped back her hair. Then she took a bite of her turkey sandwich.

"Maybe they just didn't want *Brenda*," Bess whispered.

Nancy returned to her lunch. She hoped the bad news wasn't true. But they would find out—soon enough!

After school the girls each got permission to meet at Karen Koombs's house.

7

Nancy rang the doorbell.

"What's the password?" a girl's voice called from behind the door.

"Is it lizard dance?" Nancy guessed.

The door flew wide open. Karen stood there wearing a Mr. Lizard T-shirt.

"Follow me," Karen said.

Nancy, Bess, and George followed Karen down to the basement. Nancy saw six kids sitting in front of a TV. Some were wearing Mr. Lizard T-shirts. Others wore bright red Mr. Lizard wigs.

"This is Nancy, Bess, and George," Karen said. "They knew the password."

Peter DeSands from Mrs. Reynolds's class stood up. "How do we know they're not spies?" he asked.

"Don't be silly," Nancy said. "If we were spies, would we be able to do this?"

Nancy wiggled her fingers behind her head. She flicked out her tongue. Then she, Bess, and George danced the lizard dance—perfectly.

"Wow!" Karen said, smiling. "You really *do* like Mr. Lizard!"

"That's why we want to know if the news is true," Nancy explained. "Is *Mr. Lizard's Funhouse* going off TV?"

Everyone looked very sad.

"It's true." A girl wearing a red wig sighed. "Mr. Lizard just said so himself. His last show will be on Thursday."

Karen pumped her fist in the air. "Unless we can think of a way to save Mr. Lizard," she said.

"I know!" a girl with curly hair said. "We can cross our fingers and our toes—and wish really, really hard."

"We can send station WRIV a pizza," a boy with freckles said. "And write 'Save Mr. Lizard' with pepperonis and olives."

Nancy had an idea, too. "Why don't we get all the kids who like Mr. Lizard to sign a petition?" she asked.

"A pet-what?" Peter asked.

"It's a list of names," Nancy explained. "The fifth grade started one last year when they wanted granola bars in the snack machine."

"It worked," the curly-haired girl said. "We got granola bars *and* raisins!"

"We can bring the list to station WRIV," Nancy went on. "Then they'll see how many kids really like Mr. Lizard."

"Awesome idea!" Karen declared. "Will you put together the petition, Nancy?"

"Me?" Nancy asked. She looked at Bess and George. They were nodding hard.

"Sure," Nancy said. "I'll get kids to sign it in the lunchroom tomorrow—"

Nancy was interrupted by a loud pounding on the door.

"Let me in!" a boy's voice yelled. "I want to watch *Artie the Aardvark!*"

Nancy guessed that the boy was Karen's little brother, Jimmy.

"Go away!" Karen shouted. "We're trying to save Mr. Lizard!"

"Mr. Lizard! Mr. Lizard!" Jimmy shouted. "I hope he goes away forever and ever and ever!"

Nancy's eyes opened wide.

That will never happen, she thought. Not if I can help it!

2

Nightmare for Nancy

Would anyone like to sign our petition?" Nancy asked her class in the lunchroom the next day.

"For what?" Jason Hutchings joked. "Cherry soda in the water fountains?"

"Less homework," Amara Shane said.

"More jump ropes in the schoolyard!" Molly Angelo cheered.

"No," Nancy said. "It's to keep Mr. Lizard on TV."

The kids nodded. Most of them had heard the bad news on TV the day before.

"The Mr. Lizard Fan Club gave Nancy a special job," Bess bragged.

"She's getting all the kids who like Mr. Lizard to sign their names," George added.

Nancy heard a sputter. She looked up and saw Brenda wiping tomato juice from her chin.

"The fan club let you in?" Brenda gasped. "All three of you?"

"Sure," Nancy said. "I guess they like third graders. Right, Peter?"

"Right," Peter DeSands said.

Brenda turned as red as her tomato juice. Then she seemed to force a smile.

"I'll sign the petition," Brenda said sweetly. "Anything to save Mr. Lizard."

Nancy laid the petition on the table. She had worked on it the night before.

There were three sheets of lined paper for kids to sign. On top was a colorful picture of Mr. Lizard that Karen had given her. On it Nancy had written "Save Mr. Lizard" in big black letters.

Brenda signed the petition first. Then she passed it down the table.

12

"Bess and I can get the other tables to sign in the meantime," George offered.

"Thanks," Nancy said. She handed Bess and George the other two sign-up sheets.

Mrs. Reynolds's class finished signing the petition. Nancy glanced around the lunchroom. Who would sign next?

"Keep those trays moving!" Nancy heard Mrs. Carmichael shout.

Mrs. Carmichael! Nancy thought excitedly. I'll get her to sign. She'll be our first grown-up.

Nancy carried the petition to the counter. "Hi, Mrs. Carmichael," she said.

"Hi, yourself," Mrs. Carmichael said brightly. She held up a dish. "How about some crème caramel for dessert? It's from my new cookbook."

Nancy's mouth watered at the creamy dessert. But she had work to do.

"No, thank you," Nancy said. "But would you like to sign our petition? It's to save the Mr. Lizard show."

Nancy held up the picture of Mr. Lizard.

Mrs. Carmichael's eyes opened wide. The plate in her hand shook.

"I c-can't sign that petition," Mrs. Carmichael stammered. "I won't! I refuse!"

"But—" Nancy started to say.

"Keep the line moving!" Mrs. Carmichael yelled at the top of her lungs.

Nancy was confused. Why was Mrs. Carmichael acting so strange?

Then Nancy saw a cookbook on Mrs. Carmichael's side of the counter. The name of the book was *The Clever Cook Cooks*.

So that explained it.

Mrs. Carmichael is a Clever Cook fan! Nancy thought. That's why she doesn't want to save *Mr. Lizard's Funhouse*.

Nancy spent the rest of the lunch period getting more signatures. When lunch was over she met Bess and George by their cubbies outside the classroom.

"Three pages of signatures!" Nancy cheered as they checked out the papers.

"Both sides!" George pointed out.

"Where are you going to keep the petition during class, Nancy?" Bess asked.

Nancy put the petition and picture of Mr. Lizard inside a big yellow envelope.

"It won't fit in my desk," Nancy said. "So I'll keep it inside my cubby."

Very carefully Nancy slid the envelope into her cubby. She looked over her shoulder and saw Jimmy Koombs. He was leaning on a cubby shelf and watching her.

"Mr. Lizard, Mr. Lizard," Jimmy muttered. "That's all my sister ever talks about. Blah, blah, blah, *blah!*"

"What's his problem?" George whispered to Nancy.

"Not everyone has to like Mr. Lizard." Nancy shrugged. "Just like not everyone likes chocolate ice cream."

The girls filed into the classroom. They sat down at their desks. Nancy tried to pay attention to Mrs. Reynolds, but her thoughts kept going back to the petition.

What if the envelope fell out of my cubby? Nancy wondered. Or got crushed?

Nancy wanted to make sure her envelope was safe. So when Molly needed to go to the washroom, Nancy raised her hand to be her hall buddy. Molly picked Brenda instead.

Oh, well, Nancy thought. I'm sure the envelope is just fine.

After a spelling quiz and current events, three o'clock finally arrived.

Nancy pulled the big yellow envelope from her cubby and hugged it to her chest.

"All systems go!" she announced.

Mrs. Marvin picked the girls up from school. After making a couple of stops, she drove them to the TV station in her red minivan.

"There's the fan club!" George called. She pointed out the window.

Nancy leaned over Bess and George to look out. The whole fan club was marching in front of the station. They were carrying homemade signs that read, Save Mr. Lizard!

"Wow!" Bess said. She popped the last of her chocolate bar into her mouth.

"I'll pick you girls up in an hour," Mrs. Marvin said with a smile. "Good luck!"

Nancy, Bess, and George waved to Mrs.

Marvin as she drove away. Then they ran straight to Karen.

"Three pages of signatures!" George told Karen. "Check it out!"

"No time for that," Karen said. She grabbed the envelope. "Now let's march through those doors and save Mr. Lizard!"

"Save Mr. Lizard!" the fan club chanted. "Save Mr. Lizard!"

The four girls bumped into one another as they hurried through the glass doors.

"May I help you?" a guard asked.

"Yes," Karen said. "We have something for Mr. Lizard."

A woman with dark hair and glasses was standing nearby. "I'll take it," she said. "I'm Jane, the producer of the show."

"And I'm that other guy," the man with her said with a wink. He had bright red hair.

"It's him!" Bess squealed under her breath. "It's Mr. Lizard."

"Thanks, girls!" Mr. Lizard said. He wiggled his hand behind his head.

Mr. Lizard's giant shoes thumped as he

walked down the hall. Jane followed him, carrying the big envelope.

Nancy and her friends were too excited to speak. They hurried out of the station and onto the sidewalk.

"We did it!" Karen announced to the fan club. "Thanks to Nancy!"

"Nan-cy! Nan-cy!" the kids cheered.

Nancy felt very proud—until the doors swung open and Mr. Lizard marched out. In his hand was the yellow envelope.

"What's the big idea, kids?" Mr. Lizard asked. "Is this some kind of joke?"

Nancy stared at Mr. Lizard. Why was he so angry?

Mr. Lizard reached into the envelope. He pulled out a sheet of notebook paper.

Everyone gasped. Written on it in big purple letters were the words "Get rid of Mr. Lizard!!"

Nancy's knees turned to jelly.

She didn't write that nasty note. And she had no idea who did!

3

Prove It or Else!

Now my show will be canned for sure,"
Mr. Lizard said. He gave Karen the envelope with the petition and walked back
into the station.

"How did that happen, Karen?" a girl
wearing a Mr. Lizard wig asked.

Karen handed the envelope to Nancy.
"Why don't we ask Nancy?" she said
angrily. "She was in charge!"

All eyes turned to Nancy.

"I didn't write that note!" Nancy
blurted, her eyes wide. "I wrote 'Save Mr.
Lizard' on his picture."

"Show them, Nancy," George said.

"Yeah!" Bess said. "Show them."

Nancy reached into the envelope. The three sign-up sheets were there. But the colorful picture of Mr. Lizard was gone!

"It *was* in here," Nancy said.

"I told you they were spies," Peter told Karen. "They probably work for the Clever Cook, too."

"Yeah!" A girl pointed to Bess. "That one has chocolate all over her hands!"

Bess gasped. She hid her smudgy hands behind her back.

"I don't know how the note got inside my envelope!" Nancy insisted.

"But she's going to find out," George said. "Right, Nancy?"

"Huh?" Nancy asked.

"Nancy is the best detective in school," Bess bragged to the fan club. "If anyone can find the person who wrote that nasty note, Nancy can."

"Unless *she* wrote it," Peter muttered.

"Come on, you guys," Karen told the fan club. "Let's go to my house. We can bury our Mr. Lizard wigs in my backyard."

Nancy watched as the kids left, dragging their signs behind them.

"Great." Nancy groaned. "Now everyone thinks I did it."

"Big deal," George said. "You'll show them they're wrong."

Nancy looked at the nasty note. "But where do I start?" she wondered out loud.

"Where you always do," Bess said cheerily. "In your detective notebook."

Nancy nodded. Her friends were right. It was time for another mystery.

She reached into her pocket and pulled out her notebook. A polka-dotted pencil was tucked inside.

"Let's get to work," Nancy said.

The girls sat down on a nearby bench. Nancy opened her notebook to a fresh page. On top Nancy wrote, "Who Wrote the Nasty Note?" Then she began to think.

"Someone switched the nice picture with the nasty note," Nancy said.

"But where?" Bess asked.

"Probably inside my cubby," Nancy replied. "The person had to be in the hall while we were in the classroom."

"I have a hunch," George said. "I'll bet the culprit is hiding the nice picture of Mr. Lizard somewhere."

"That's a good hunch!" Nancy said. She wrote the thought in her notebook. Then she looked at the nasty note again.

"Whoever wrote this," Nancy said, "must own a purple marker."

Bess ran her finger across the "Get rid of Mr. Lizard" message. "And he or she doesn't like Mr. Lizard," she said sadly.

"Who wouldn't like Mr. Lizard?" George asked.

"Jimmy Koombs," Nancy remembered. "He wanted Mr. Lizard to go away forever."

"And he saw you put the petition inside your cubby," George pointed out.

"But how could Jimmy have gotten into your cubby?" Bess asked.

"Easy," Nancy said. "He could have left his class to get a drink of water."

Nancy wrote the word "Suspects" on the

next page. Then she wrote Jimmy Koombs's name right under it.

"Jimmy didn't sign the petition either," Bess remembered. "When I asked the first graders, he sat on his hands."

Nancy suddenly remembered another person who wouldn't sign the petition.

"Mrs. Carmichael refused to sign, too," Nancy said. "And she had a copy of the Clever Cook's cookbook."

"You mean all those yummy lunches were the Clever Cook's?" Bess cried.

"The enemy has wormed his way into our lunchroom!" George said with narrowed eyes.

Just then Nancy thought of something.

"Mrs. Carmichael uses a purple marker to write her lunches each week," she said.

"But Mrs. Carmichael is nice," Bess said. "Why would she ruin our petition?"

"My dad told me that sometimes people do things without thinking," Nancy said.

Bess and George nodded. Mr. Drew was a lawyer. He often gave Nancy good advice.

Nancy added Mrs. Carmichael's name to her list of suspects. She was glad to have two suspects. But she was also worried.

"The school has hundreds of kids." Nancy sighed. *"Anyone* could have done it."

"Nancy, look!" Bess cried.

Nancy turned to see where Bess was pointing. A bald man carrying a cardboard box was leaving the station.

"That's Mr. Lizard," George hissed. "Without his red wig."

The girls ran over to Mr. Lizard.

"Isn't it supposed to be a secret that your hair is fake?" George asked Mr. Lizard.

"What difference does it make?" Mr. Lizard groaned. "Soon I'll be flipping burgers and wearing a hairnet."

Nancy stared at the box in Mr. Lizard's arms. A giant shoe stuck out.

"You're not cleaning out your dressing room, are you?" Nancy asked.

"Sure," Mr. Lizard said. "I've got to make room for the Clever Crook—I mean Cook."

"We're sorry about that nasty message, Mr. Lizard," Nancy said.

"Too late," Mr. Lizard said. "The president of the TV station saw it. Now she thinks you all want to get rid of me."

"No!" Bess cried, waving her arms.

"The petition really said *'Save* Mr. Lizard,'" George insisted. "And Nancy here is going to prove it."

"How?" Mr. Lizard asked.

"For starters," Nancy said, "can you think of anyone who may not like you?"

"Just one kid," Mr. Lizard said. "He wanted to come on my show with his science project. But I told him no."

"Who was it?" Nancy asked.

"It's no use, kids." Mr. Lizard sighed. He dumped the box into a trash can. "The Clever Cook is coming to the station in two days. Then I'm history."

Mr. Lizard wiggled his fingers behind his head. Then he walked away.

"I'm never eating the Clever Cook's lunches again," Bess said, pouting. "I'll eat tuna sandwiches—till I grow gills!"

The girls walked to the trash can. They stared at Mr. Lizard's cardboard box.

Next to the giant shoe was a brown folder. Nancy pulled it out. The white label on the folder read, "Nasty Mail."

"Bess, George!" Nancy said excitedly. "I think we just found some more clues!"

4

Ice Scream

"It's not polite to read other people's mail," Bess said as Nancy opened the folder with Mr. Lizard's mail.

"It's not polite to send nasty letters either," George told Bess.

Nancy pulled out three letters. Each had been written on a computer. They were on the same stationery—blue and white with a black insect design.

"Phooey!" George said. "None of the letters are signed."

"But the letters are on the same stationery," Nancy said. "That means they probably came from the same person."

Each girl took a letter. Each read hers out loud.

"'Dear Mr. Lizard,'" Nancy read. "'You are like mold growing on stinky cheese.'"

"'Mr. Lizard,'" Bess read. "'I hope you grow a fungus on your big toe.'"

Bess turned to Nancy and George. "What's a fungus?" she asked.

"Something yucky," George said. She began to read her letter. "'Mr. Lizard. 'Eat ants for breakfast!'"

"Eww!" Bess said. "Those letters aren't just nasty—they're gross!"

"Mold . . . fungus . . . ants," Nancy said slowly. "Hmm. Those were all part of Dalton Feivish's past science projects."

Nancy pulled out the petition and looked for Dalton's name.

"Aha!" Nancy said. "Dalton didn't sign the petition either. Which probably means he doesn't like Mr. Lizard!"

"Because Mr. Lizard wouldn't let him bring his science project on the show!" George said, snapping her fingers.

"Now you have three suspects, Nancy," Bess said happily.

"And if Dalton has a purple marker," Nancy added, "he'll be my number *one* suspect."

The girls ran back to Mr. Lizard's cardboard box for more clues. George pulled out the pair of giant shoes.

"George!" Bess cried. "You're not going to wear those, are you?"

"Nope," George said. "I'm saving them for Mr. Lizard. He's going to need them when he goes back on TV."

Nancy heard a car horn honk. She turned and saw Mrs. Marvin pulling up in her red minivan.

"Well?" Mrs. Marvin asked the girls. "Did you save *Mr. Lizard's Funhouse?*"

"Not yet, Mom," Bess said. "But we're working on it."

"Then how about working on some ice-cream sundaes at the Double Dip?" Mrs. Marvin asked.

"Cool!" Nancy, Bess, and George cried at

the same time. The Double Dip had the best ice cream in River Heights.

The girls chatted about the case inside the minivan. But when they reached the Double Dip their thoughts turned to their favorite flavors—strawberry, rocky road, and mint chocolate chip.

Mrs. Marvin lined up at the register to pay. The girls carried their dishes of ice cream to a round table.

"I wonder if the Clever Cook has recipes for ice cream," George said.

"If he does," Bess said, "they're probably stuffed with hard-boiled eggs."

"Yuck—gross!" Nancy complained.

"Speaking of gross," George said. "Look who's sitting across the parlor."

Nancy looked over her shoulder.

Dalton Feivish was sitting alone at a table. He had a dish of vanilla ice cream in front of him. But instead of eating it he was staring at it.

"Dalton Feivish!" George whispered. "Are we lucky or what?"

"And look!" Nancy whispered. "Dalton's

backpack is next to his foot. That's probably where he keeps his pencils and pens."

"And purple markers," Bess whispered.

The girls stood up from their table. They walked over to Dalton.

"Hi, Dalton," Nancy said.

"Silence!" Dalton ordered. "I'm in the middle of an experiment. I'm seeing how long it takes ice cream to melt."

"What's so great about that?" George asked.

"I sprinkled it with pepper and onion powder," Dalton said. "And a dash of my own spit."

"Ewww!" Bess cried.

Nancy was grossed out, too. But she had to talk to Dalton.

"What a cool experiment, Dalton," Nancy said. "Maybe you should show it on TV. Like maybe . . . *Mr. Lizard's Funhouse?*"

Dalton squeezed his hands into fists. He pounded the table. "Don't ever mention Mr. Lizard to me again!" he shouted.

The girls exchanged glances.

"Now if you'll excuse me," Dalton said, "I must focus. In the name of science!"

Dalton narrowed his eyes. He continued to stare at the ice cream.

The girls stepped back from the table. Nancy could see Mrs. Marvin waving to them from their table.

"In a minute, Mom!" Bess called.

"Dalton *is* mad at Mr. Lizard," Nancy whispered. "So he might have written those letters."

"The nasty note, too," George said. "I wonder if he has a purple marker."

Nancy looked at Dalton's backpack. A red plastic case with tiny holes was sticking out of one pocket.

"Look!" Nancy said. She pointed to the backpack. "Dalton probably keeps his pens and pencils in that red case."

George brought her finger to her lips. She tiptoed quietly to Dalton's table. Dalton was still staring at his ice cream when George pulled out the red case.

George hurried back to Nancy. She winked as she handed her the case.

Nancy gave George a thank-you smile. But when she opened the plastic case she gasped.

The case wasn't filled with pencils, pens, or even purple markers. It was filled with soggy soil, apple slices, and—

"Worms!" Nancy cried.

5

The Pumped-Up Purple Print

"Eek!" Bess shrieked when she saw the worms.

Nancy jumped. She tossed the case with the worms to George.

"I don't want it!" George cried. She tossed the case to Bess. Bess shrieked even louder and dropped it on the floor.

Nancy gulped. The case snapped open, and the worms came crawling out. Other customers jumped up and screamed as the worms wiggled this way and that.

"Look what you did!" Dalton cried. He got down on his knees and began scooping up the worms. "My worm farm is my next great science project!"

"You mean gross!" George said.

Nancy took a deep breath. Then she and George kneeled on the floor and helped scoop up the worms. Bess stood on the side with her eyes squeezed shut.

"What is going on here?" Mrs. Marvin demanded as she walked over.

"Sorry, Mom," Bess said. "It was an accident."

"Thanks to you!" Dalton said. He shut the lid of his red case with a snap.

Cathy Perez, the owner of the Double Dip, marched over, too. "I'm afraid you kids will have to leave," she said. "And please don't bring bugs in here again."

"They're not bugs," Dalton said as they left. "They're earthworms."

While Mrs. Marvin got the minivan, the kids waited outside the Double Dip.

"Why were you going through my things anyway?" Dalton asked the girls.

Nancy explained all about the petition and the "Get Rid of Mr. Lizard" message.

And about the purple marker they thought he had.

"I *am* mad at Mr. Lizard," Dalton admitted. "He wouldn't let me bring my stinky cheese experiment on his show."

"So it was you!" Nancy cried.

"He said my project was too gross," Dalton went on. "Even for his show."

"So you wrote him nasty letters?" Nancy asked with a frown.

Dalton nodded.

"But I didn't mess up your petition," he said. "I wasn't even in school this afternoon. I was at the dentist."

Nancy tilted her head to study Dalton. Was he telling the truth?

"If you don't believe me," Dalton said, "you can ask my mom."

"Did someone say my name?" a cheery voice called.

Nancy turned. She saw a dark-haired woman carrying two shopping bags.

"Tell them, Mom," Dalton said. "Tell them where I was this afternoon."

"Oh, Dalton was at the dentist," Mrs.

Feivish said. She shook her finger at Dalton. "He's been eating too many of those worms lately."

"Eating worms?" the girls shrieked.

"*Gummy* worms," Dalton said, rolling his eyes. "Du-uh!"

Nancy watched as Dalton and his mom walked away. She took out her notebook and crossed off Dalton's name.

"Now we're left with Jimmy Koombs and Mrs. Carmichael," Nancy said.

"Should we go to the Koombses' house now?" Bess asked. "I can ask my mom to drive us there."

"We can check on Jimmy at school tomorrow," Nancy said. "Let's just go home."

"Good," George said. "Because today was the pits. First the petition. Then the worms—"

"And worst of all," Bess said. "We never got to finish our ice cream!"

Mrs. Marvin drove Nancy home. After doing her math homework Nancy joined her father at the dinner table.

"I think you'll like dinner tonight," Hannah Gruen said. "It's stuffed shells with three kinds of cheeses."

"Yum!" Nancy said.

Hannah had been the Drews' housekeeper since Nancy was three years old.

"I got the recipe from a new cookbook," Hannah went on. "It's called *The Clever Cook Cooks*."

Nancy jumped in her chair. "Th-th-the Clever Cook?" she stammered.

"What's wrong, Pudding Pie?" Mr. Drew asked Nancy.

Nancy took a deep breath. Then she explained everything about her new case.

"Now I have to find out who switched the nice picture of Mr. Lizard with that creepy message," Nancy said.

"This should help," Mr. Drew said. He reached under his jacket and pulled out a big silver magnifying glass. "A good detective never leaves home without it."

Nancy smiled at her surprise gift. The magnifying glass would be perfect for seeing small things up close.

"Thanks, Daddy!" Nancy said. She took the magnifying glass and held it over her fork. It looked as big as a pitchfork!

"Now," Hannah said, "will you be eating the Clever Cook's dish? Or can I interest you in a peanut butter sandwich?"

Nancy looked at the steaming hot shells bubbling with cheese.

"Stuffed shells, please." Nancy sighed. "Oh, Hannah. Why does the Clever Cook have to be so *good?*"

After a great dinner, Nancy took her new magnifying glass upstairs to her room. Her chocolate Labrador puppy, Chocolate Chip, lay on the floor while Nancy sat at her desk and studied the note.

"Hmm," Nancy said, peering through the glass. "The letters are bigger, but they're still the same."

"Woof!" Chip barked, and jumped onto Nancy's lap. That made Nancy drop the note on the rug.

"Chip!" Nancy complained. "Look what you made me do."

Nancy reached for the note. It was facing

down. Near the corner of the paper was something Nancy hadn't noticed before—a bright purple smudge.

Nancy leaned over her bed and looked through her magnifying glass. The purple smudge wasn't just a smudge.

"It's a fingerprint!" Nancy gasped. "A bright purple fingerprint!"

And a great new clue!

6

Jimmy on the Run

My dad said everyone's fingerprints are different," Nancy told Bess and George. "So this one should lead us right to the culprit."

It was Wednesday morning. The girls were walking through the hall to their classroom. Nancy carried her new magnifying glass in her backpack.

"But first," Nancy went on, "we have to match this fingerprint with our suspects' fingerprints."

"I know a way we can get Jimmy Koombs's fingerprints," Bess said. "Just look at one of his finger paintings."

"First graders don't finger paint anymore," George said.

"Then let's hope Jimmy has messy hands," Nancy said with a sigh.

The girls walked some more. Then Nancy stopped in front of the lunchroom. Mrs. Carmichael was kneeling under a table and wiping something off the floor.

"I'll bet Mrs. Carmichael's fingerprints are all over the kitchen," Nancy said. "Too bad we can't search it."

"Who says we can't?" George said with a sly smile. "Follow me."

Nancy's heart pounded as they sneaked past Mrs. Carmichael into the kitchen.

"That was close!" Nancy whispered. She looked around the kitchen. On the counter next to a big bowl of flour was a flat slab of dough.

"It's probably full of Mrs. Carmichael's fingerprints," Nancy said.

She pulled out her magnifying glass and held it over the dough.

"Any fingerprints?" George asked.

"No." Nancy sighed. "Mrs. Carmichael was probably wearing rubber gloves."

"Ooh!" Bess said, leaning over the counter. "This bowl of flour smells yummy. Like sugar and lemons."

Bess held the bowl up to her face. She took a giant whiff. Then she threw back her head and began to sneeze.

"Ah-ah-ah-choooo!"

Poof! The flour blew out of the bowl and covered the girls' faces.

"Yuck!" Nancy said, wiping the white flour from her eyelids.

"We look like ghosts!" Bess cried.

Nancy gulped when she saw an angry Mrs. Carmichael standing in the doorway.

"Good grief!" Mrs. Carmichael cried. "What are you girls doing in my kitchen?"

"Oh, great," Nancy groaned under her breath. But she bravely explained everything—the nasty note, the purple marker, and the fingerprint.

"Let me see that note," Mrs. Carmichael said.

Nancy held up the note with the purple

47

fingerprint. She expected Mrs. Carmichael to be mad, but instead she smiled.

"Look at this," Mrs. Carmichael said. She held her hand up to the purple fingerprint. "My fingers are much, much bigger than this print."

Nancy compared Mrs. Carmichael's fingers to the fingerprint. They *were* much bigger.

"Now check out my purple marker," Mrs. Carmichael said. She pulled out her marker and drew a line on a paper napkin.

Nancy compared the two purples. The purple on the napkin was reddish purple. The purple on the note was a bluish purple.

"They *are* different," Nancy admitted. "I guess you didn't write that note after all, Mrs. Carmichael."

"And I never would," Mrs. Carmichael said. "I had a favorite show when I was a kid, too. It was called the *Mr. Funny Bones Show.* I used to rush home every day after school to watch it."

Nancy felt bad for suspecting Mrs.

Carmichael. But she had to follow up on her clues.

"We're sorry for sneaking into your kitchen," Nancy told Mrs. Carmichael.

"Don't worry," Mrs. Carmichael said. "I would have done anything to save Mr. Funny Bones, too."

Mrs. Carmichael helped Nancy, Bess, and George clean their faces. Then the girls hurried to their classroom.

"Now our only suspect is Jimmy Koombs," Bess said.

"Let's search Jimmy's cubby," Nancy said. "If he took the picture of Mr. Lizard, he might have stuck it in there."

The girls walked down the hall to the first-grade cubbies. They were all empty.

"The first grade went on a field trip to a cupcake factory," a second-grade boy told them. "Lucky ducks!"

Nancy didn't feel very lucky. She walked with Bess and George to their own cubbies. She was about to put her lunch inside when she saw Brenda.

"I heard what happened yesterday," Brenda said with a mean smile. "Thanks to you, the Mr. Lizard show is history."

Nancy watched Brenda hold up a notebook with colorful butterflies on the cover.

"And I'm writing all about it in my newspaper!" Brenda said. She flipped her dark hair over her shoulder and strutted into the classroom.

"Great," Nancy groaned. "Now Brenda is going to blame me in the *Carlton News!*"

"You mean the *Carlton Pe-ews*," George joked.

"Come on, Nancy," Bess said. She headed toward the classroom door. "We'll find Jimmy after school."

The day went by quickly. Nancy and her class learned new vocabulary words. In arts and crafts they made collages out of autumn leaves.

After school Nancy ran home for a snack. Then Hannah gave her permission to walk Chip. Bess and George were waiting outside to join her.

"Let's walk Chip straight to Jimmy's house," Nancy told her friends.

Chip stopped to sniff some fallen leaves on the way. When the three friends reached the Koombses' house Nancy handed Chip's leash to Bess. Then she rang the doorbell.

The curtain on the door window shifted slightly. Karen peeked out.

"Go away!" Karen called out. "We're having our last fan club meeting. And you've caused enough trouble."

"But, Karen," Nancy pleaded. "I have to speak to Jimmy!"

"The password is NO!" Karen snapped. She let the curtain fall and she was gone.

"Now we'll have to wait until tomorrow to talk to Jimmy," Nancy said.

"Not exactly," George whispered. She grinned and pointed over Nancy's shoulder.

Nancy whirled around. Jimmy was sneaking around the side of the house.

A backpack dangled from Jimmy's shoulder as he made his way to the sidewalk. Nancy saw a colorful picture sticking out. The top part of the picture showed a mop of bright red hair.

"Bess! George!" Nancy cried. "Jimmy has a picture of Mr. Lizard in his backpack. And I'll bet it's mine!"

7

Scratch or Catch?

Stop!" Nancy shouted to Jimmy.

Jimmy looked over his shoulder at Nancy. But instead of stopping, he began to run. Faster and faster.

"Let's get him!" George said.

All three girls and Chip ran after Jimmy. But Jimmy was way ahead of them.

"How can such a little boy run so fast?" George asked as they ran.

"How can a *puppy* run so fast?" Bess puffed as she ran behind Chip.

The girls chased Jimmy down the block and around a corner. Nancy could see Chip pulling at her leash. She gave such a hard tug that she yanked the leash from Bess's hand.

"Sorry, Nancy!" Bess wailed as Chip charged after Jimmy.

"Chip—stop!" Nancy shouted.

Chip caught up with Jimmy. She jumped up and tugged playfully at his backpack with her teeth.

"Let go!" Jimmy yelped.

Chip yanked the backpack off Jimmy's shoulder. It fell to the ground. A bunch of pictures scattered all over the sidewalk!

"Wow!" George cried as the girls caught up to Jimmy and Chip. "They're all of Mr. Lizard."

"And they're all messed up," Bess said, shaking her head.

Nancy looked down at the pictures. Mr. Lizard's teeth were blacked out. His eyes were drawn to look crossed.

But that wasn't all. Written in red crayon on the bottom of each picture was, "Misstir Lizzerd stinks!"

"Where did you get all those pictures?" Nancy asked Jimmy.

"My lips are zipped!" Jimmy said. He pretended to zipper his lips shut.

Chip wagged her tail. She jumped up on Jimmy and began licking his face.

"Help!" Jimmy yelled. "I'm drowning in dog spit. Get her off!"

"Not until you tell us where you got these pictures," Nancy said.

"Okay," Jimmy said. "I took them from my sister's fan club box. I was going to hang them up all over River Heights."

"That's mean!" Nancy scolded. She gently pulled Chip off Jimmy.

"And I'll bet you messed up Nancy's petition, too!" Bess declared.

"What are you talking about?" Jimmy asked. "I didn't even sign that list."

Nancy picked up a picture. She studied it closely. Then she waved Bess and George to the side.

"Jimmy didn't write the nasty purple message," Nancy whispered.

"How do you know?" George asked.

Nancy pointed to "Misstir Lizzerd stinks." "Jimmy can't even *spell* Mr. Lizard," she pointed out.

"Oh, yeah," Bess said.

The girls walked back to Jimmy.

"Promise that you'll never hang up these pictures, Jimmy," Nancy said.

"No way!" Jimmy said angrily.

"Then I'll tell Karen," Nancy said. "And she'll never let you watch *Artie the Aardvark* again."

"N-no Artie?" Jimmy stammered. He looked at the pictures and sighed. "Okay, okay. Mr. Lizard is history anyway."

The words hit Nancy like a ton of bricks. Jimmy was right. The next day was Thursday—Mr. Lizard's last day.

And I have no more suspects, Nancy thought sadly. Zero. Zip. Zilch!

"I feel like a total loser, Daddy," Nancy told her father during dinner that night. "All my clues led me to the wrong suspects."

"Don't give up, Nancy," Hannah said as she poured Nancy a glass of milk. "You never do."

"Hannah's right," Mr. Drew said. "There may be more to your clues than meets the eye."

Nancy took a sip of milk. What did her father mean by that?

When Nancy finished her chicken casserole she excused herself from the table. Chocolate Chip followed Nancy up the stairs to her room.

"More than meets the eye," Nancy repeated out loud. She opened her detective notebook. The nasty note fell out on her bed.

"I've looked at this a hundred times, Chip!" Nancy complained. She grabbed her magnifying glass and sighed. "Here goes a hundred and one."

Chip grunted softly as Nancy held the magnifying glass over the message. She moved it up and down until the words, "Get rid of Mr. Lizard," were as big as could be.

"Now what?" Nancy muttered.

But when she moved the magnifying glass closer she noticed something else. There were marks on the paper as if someone had written on another piece of paper on top of that one.

Nancy ran to her desk. She held the paper under her lamp. But she couldn't tell what the marks were. Words? Pictures? Or just doodles?

Nancy looked up and saw a box of crayons on her desk. It made her think of an old detective trick that her father had once taught her.

"That's it!" Nancy said. She pulled out a dark green crayon. Then she colored lightly over the marks. The paper turned green but the marks stayed white.

Soon the scratches became letters. And the letters became words.

"*The Carlton News* by Brenda Carlton,'" Nancy read. She looked up. "Brenda?"

Suddenly it clicked.

"Brenda and Molly went to the washroom," Nancy said excitedly. "The same afternoon the nasty note appeared in my envelope!"

Chip gave a low growl.

Nancy wanted to growl, too. Did the nasty message come from Brenda's butterfly notebook?

8

Miss Snooty Pants
Strikes Again!

Brenda Carlton!" George said, shaking her head. "Why didn't we suspect her before?"

"Probably because Brenda likes Mr. Lizard," Nancy said. "And she did sign the petition."

It was Thursday morning. Nancy had just shown her friends the scratchy message in the schoolyard.

"But how could Molly let Brenda do such a mean thing?" Bess asked.

Nancy decided to ask Molly. They found her by the water fountain.

"Think back to Tuesday, Molly," Nancy said. "When you went to the washroom with Brenda—"

"Brenda never came with me to the washroom," Molly interrupted. "She said she had to get something from her cubby."

"Was Brenda at the cubbies all that time?" Nancy asked Molly.

Molly shook her head. "Brenda came to the washroom just as I was leaving," she said. "She had to wash some icky purple stuff off her hands."

"Purple?" Bess gasped.

"Brenda Carlton is guilty!" George declared.

"Not yet," Nancy said. "We have to question her—and find that purple pen."

Molly tilted her head and smiled. "Is this another mystery?" she asked.

"Isn't it always?" Bess giggled.

The school bell rang. Nancy, Bess, and George headed straight to their cubbies.

Nancy saw Brenda pushing her backpack into her cubby. She decided to get right to the point.

"Tell the truth, Brenda," Nancy said. "Did you switch the nice picture of Mr. Lizard with the nasty note?"

Brenda straightened up. She looked Nancy in the eye. "Why would I do that?" she asked. "I watch Mr. Lizard, too."

"Because you were in the hall when the picture was switched," George said.

"May we look inside your pencil case, Brenda?" Nancy asked.

"No way!" Brenda said. She reached for her backpack. But when she pulled it from her cubby something else slid out. It was a picture of Mr. Lizard with the words "Save Mr. Lizard" on the bottom.

"It's my picture!" Nancy declared.

"I don't know how it got there," Brenda blurted. "And if you think I wrote that nasty note—you're wrong!"

"Maybe," Nancy said. She pulled the note from her own backpack and pointed to the purple smudge. "But fingerprints never lie. They're like snowflakes—all different."

"Fingerprints?" Brenda gasped. She hid her hands behind her back.

"Well, Brenda?" Nancy demanded. "Did you . . . or didn't you?"

Brenda's eyes narrowed. She heaved a big sigh. Then she pulled a purple marker from her backpack.

"This was in my pocket when I went to the washroom," Brenda said. "So was a piece of paper from my notebook."

"You planned the whole thing," George said angrily.

"Why did you want to hurt Mr. Lizard, Brenda?" Nancy asked.

"It wasn't Mr. Lizard I was trying to hurt," Brenda said. "It was you!"

"Me?" Nancy asked.

"I was mad that the fan club gave you a special job," Brenda explained. "They wouldn't even let me join."

"So you tried to make me look bad?" Nancy asked.

"I guess," Brenda said. Her shoulders drooped. "What I did was horrible. But I want to make it up to you. Really!"

"How?" Nancy asked.

"Let's go to the TV station after school," Brenda suggested. "I'll apologize. And tell everyone that your petition really said 'Save Mr. Lizard.'"

Nancy felt Bess and George pull her aside. They formed a huddle and whispered.

"How can we trust Brenda, Nancy?" George asked. "She's lied before."

"What if she's just being Brenda-ish again?" Bess whispered.

"We *have* to trust her," Nancy said. "Today is Mr. Lizard's last day. There's no time!"

The girls walked back to Brenda. "It's a deal," Nancy said.

During the busy school day Nancy was happy she had solved the case. But she would be even happier when Brenda confessed to the TV station.

After school Hannah agreed to drive Nancy, Bess, and George to station WRIV.

"I'll park the car," Hannah said as the

girls stepped out. "Why don't you meet me inside?"

"Okay, Hannah," Nancy said. She turned and saw Brenda standing by her bicycle. Her arms were crossed.

"What are we waiting for?" Brenda asked. "Let's save the Mr. Lizard show!"

The four girls walked through the glass doors.

"We'd like to see Mr. Lizard, please," Brenda told the guard.

"Sure." The guard smiled. "I'll bet Mr. Lizard would like to say goodbye to his fans."

The guard led the girls to a door. She knocked and whisked them through.

Nancy looked around. Sitting behind a desk was a woman with silver hair. Standing next to the desk was Mr. Lizard; his producer, Jane; and a man with rosy cheeks, a white apron, and a chef's hat.

The Clever Cook! Nancy thought.

"Can I help you, girls?" Jane asked.

"Brenda has something to say," Nancy said. "It's about *Mr. Lizard's Funhouse*."

The silver-haired woman smiled. "She can tell me," she said. "I'm Kate Romano, the president of station WRIV."

"Go ahead, Brenda," George whispered.

But Brenda didn't apologize. Instead she stuck out her chin and smiled slyly.

"I'm not saying a word!" she said.

Nancy froze.

Brenda had lied about apologizing just to be bratty. To be Brenda-ish!

"Brenda Carlton, that's not fair!" Nancy complained.

Mr. Lizard turned to Brenda.

"Brenda Carlton?" he asked. "Aren't you the kid who writes her own newspaper?"

"That's me!" Brenda said proudly.

Mr. Lizard frowned.

"You once wrote that my hair was fake," he said. "That wasn't very nice."

"B-but—" Brenda stammered.

"What she *did* wasn't very nice either," Nancy said.

"What did she do?" Jane asked.

Everyone listened while Nancy explained

68

everything. When she was finished, Ms. Romano looked concerned.

"Oh, dear!" Ms. Romano said. "You kids went through all that trouble to save Mr. Lizard?"

Nancy, Bess, and George nodded.

"Cheese and crackers!" the Clever Cook boomed. "I didn't know I was replacing someone the kids like so much!"

"We like you, too, Mr. Cook," Nancy said. "Our lunch lady has been serving your recipes in school all week long."

"They're awesome," George said. "Like the tuna in those puffy pastry shells."

"And the stuffed eggs with mush-rooms!" Bess exclaimed. "Yum!"

"You mean kids like my recipes?" the Clever Cook asked.

The girls nodded again.

"Ms. Romano," the Clever Cook said. "Don't take Mr. Lizard off the air. Instead let me come on the show every week. I'll show the kids how they can make simple snacks with their moms and dads."

"And housekeepers," Nancy added.

"A cooking segment on *Mr. Lizard's Funhouse*," Ms. Romano said. "I like it."

"Me, too," Mr. Lizard said. "Maybe I'll finally learn how to cook fudge."

"And maybe I'll learn how to dance the lizard dance," the Clever Cook said. "From now on we're a team!"

"Does this mean the Mr. Lizard show is saved?" Nancy asked hopefully.

"Thanks to your petition," Ms. Romano said. "And the nice things you said about the Clever Cook."

Mr. Lizard held up his hands.

"Whoa—hold everything!" he said. "I can't do my show again."

"Why not?" Jane asked.

"I threw out my giant shoes," Mr. Lizard confessed.

"Don't worry." George smiled. "We saved your show—*and* your shoes!"

"Thanks, kids!" Mr. Lizard said.

Brenda cleared her throat.

"I like *Mr. Lizard's Funhouse*, too, you know," Brenda said coolly. "I even signed the petition. Didn't I, Nancy?"

Nancy stuck her chin in the air. "I'm not saying a word!" she said with a grin.

"Ooh!" Brenda said angrily. She almost bumped into Hannah as she stormed out of the office.

Hannah was thrilled to meet the Clever Cook. But after they all danced the lizard dance, it was time to go home.

Bess and George chatted excitedly in the car. But Nancy had work to do. She had to write in her blue detective notebook:

Yippee! Today I solved the case and saved *Mr. Lizard's Funhouse,* too.

The Clever Cook really is clever. He knows that teamwork is the best work of all. But the best team in the whole world will always be—Bess, George, and me!

Case closed.

EASY TO READ–FUN TO SOLVE!

**Meet up with suspense and mystery
in The Hardy Boys® are:**

THE CLUES™ BROTHERS

Available from Minstrel® Books
Published by Pocket Books

Sabrina
The Teenage Witch®

Salem's Tails®

What's it like to be a powerful warlock,
sentenced to one hundred years in a
cat's body for trying to take over the world?

Ask Salem.

**Read all about Salem's magical
adventures in this series based on the hit
ABC-TV show!**

A MINSTREL® BOOK
Published by Pocket Books

2007-12